ALLEY & Rex

ALLEY & Rex

written by
JOEL ROSS

illustrated by
NICOLE MILES

Atheneum Books for Young Readers
NEW YORK LONDON TORONTO SYDNEY NEW DELHI

A
atheneum

ATHENEUM BOOKS FOR YOUNG READERS • An imprint of Simon & Schuster Children's Publishing Division • 1230 Avenue of the Americas, New York, New York 10020 • This book is a work of fiction. Any references to historical events, real people, or real places are used fictitiously. Other names, characters, places, and events are products of the author's imagination, and any resemblance to actual events or places or persons, living or dead, is entirely coincidental. • Text © 2021 by Joel Ross • Illustration © 2021 by Nicole Miles • Jacket design © 2021 by Simon & Schuster, Inc. • All rights reserved, including the right of reproduction in whole or in part in any form. • ATHENEUM BOOKS FOR YOUNG READERS is a registered trademark of Simon & Schuster, Inc. Atheneum logo is a trademark of Simon & Schuster, Inc. • For information about special discounts for bulk purchases, please contact Simon & Schuster Special Sales at 1-866-506-1949 or business@simonandschuster.com. • The Simon & Schuster Speakers Bureau can bring authors to your live event. For more information or to book an event, contact the Simon & Schuster Speakers Bureau at 1-866-248-3049 or visit our website at www.simonspeakers.com. • The text for this book was set in Aldus. • The illustrations for this book were rendered digitally. • Manufactured in the United States of America • 0821 FFG • First Edition • 10 9 8 7 6 5 4 3 2 1 • Library of Congress Cataloging-in-Publication Data • Names: Ross, Joel N., 1968– author. | Miles, Nicole, illustrator. • Title: Alley & Rex / Joel Ross ; illustrated by Nicole Miles. • Other titles: Alley and Rex • Description: First edition. | New York : Atheneum Books for Young Readers, [2021] | Audience: Ages 8 to 12. | Summary: Sixth-grader Alley Katz must get an A on a science test, but rather than work with peer mentor Rex, a fourth grader in a bunny suit, he decides to steal the answer key from the teachers' lounge. • Identifiers: LCCN 2020042996 | ISBN 9781534495432 (hardcover) | ISBN 9781534495463 (ebook) • Subjects: CYAC: Schools—Fiction. | Behavior—Fiction. | Individuality—Fiction. | Friendship—Fiction. | Humorous stories. • Classification: LCC PZ7.1.R677 All 2021 | DDC [Fic]—dc23 • LC record available at https://lccn.loc.gov/2020042996

To the memory of my mother,
who read an early draft and said,
"So, nu? What's my Bubbie/Blatt ratio?"
90/10, Mom.

—J. R.

To Mum and Dad, and especially Dyl

—N. M.

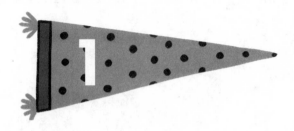

This is Blueberry Hill School, home of the Ladybugs. Look at the ordinary trees. Look at the ordinary buses.

Look at the ordinary kids.

Well, not that one.

Look at the ordinary clouds and crowds and flagpole.

Now zoom in.

My name is Alex Katz and I don't make good choices.

At least, that's what my parents and teachers say . . . if they catch me.

After I slide down the flagpole, I blend into a crowd of fourth graders heading for the front doors. I'm a sixth-grade shape-shifter, blending into the background.

Stealthy.

Hidden.

Invisible.

I'm home free!

Then I hear a laugh. A mean, mocking laugh.

It's Cameron Sykes! He's in the seventh grade. When he became a hall monitor, he turned into the King of the Snitches. These days, he spends all his time:

     1) patrolling the hallways wearing
        a homemade *#security* badge.
     2) marching around grunting,
        "Hut, hut, hut . . ."
     3) ratting on anyone who brings a
        phone to school.

4) posting embarrassing pictures of
late kids to the school website.

Also, he once threw a grapefruit at me for running in the hallway. On cold days, I can still feel the juice stinging my eye.

And now he's picking on a little kid in a bunny suit. That's not a huge surprise. Cameron is a bully, and everyone knows you can't wear an adorable rabbit onesie to school unless it's Wear an Adorable Rabbit Onesie to School Day.

Which, if you check the calendar, it never is.

So I pause for a second to explain that we shouldn't pick on littler kids . . .

. . . and from across the yard, Principal Kugelmeyer yells, "Alley!"

Which is me, because nobody calls me Alex. How I got the nickname "Alley" Katz is a long story, though. You wouldn't believe me if I told you.

"It's only the third day of school," Principal Kugelmeyer says, after dragging me into her office. "Why were you climbing the flagpole?"

"It's a tradition," I tell her. "Like the Hill Build."

My school goes from kindergarten through eighth grade. Every year, the new third graders make a model of Blueberry Hill for the Hill Build Contest. For example, when I was a little kid, I convinced my class to slather blueberry jam onto a mound of helium balloons. It was awesome. Well, it didn't look anything like the school . . . but three years later, you can still see the stains on the ceiling. I call that a win.

"Nobody ever climbed the flagpole before," Principal Kugelmeyer tells me.

"That's because it's a *new* tradition," I inform her.

"And I don't want them to start now," she

continues, bulldozing over my excellent point. "You know the other kids copy you. Especially when you do something reckless like climbing the flagpole—which is not a tradition."

"It *could* be. All traditions have to start somewhere."

Think about it. A hundred years ago, some kids dressed in costumes FOR ABSOLUTELY NO REASON and pounded on a neighbor's door, demanding candy.

The neighbor must've been like, "What art thou doing?" which is how they talked back then.

Then the kids said, "We art making a brandenew tradition called Halloween! Now hand over some Thrice Musketeers Bars, thou dorkfish, or with our TP shall we festoon thy house."

I explain that to Principal Kugelmeyer, but she's not interested in history. Honestly, I don't know how these people keep their jobs.

"This is your one free pass," she tells me, drumming her fingers on her desk. "In honor of the new school year."

"Oh! Well, um, I hope you're sitting down—"

"I *am* sitting down, Alley," she says.

"—because I just thought of a way to honor the school year *ten times more*!"

"By giving you ten free passes?"

I gape at her. How did she guess?

"Alley," she says.

"Here," I report. "Present!"

"This is your only chance. After last year . . ." She shudders. "You've been warned."

"I didn't know the crickets would do that."

She exhales. "Just remember what we said about making better choices."

"I will," I promise.

And I'll keep that vow, because I have a . . .

Last year, I made a few bad choices (also, I learned that you can order thousands of live crickets online) and almost got expelled.

So this year, I'll make *lots* of choices. Dozens and dozens of choices. That way, I'm sure to make some good ones, which will balance things out.

See? Foolproof!

Except Principal Kugelmeyer says, "I'm glad to hear that, Alley. And I'm calling your parents in for a talk, to make sure you don't forget."

That's why my dad meets me after school, in the principal's office. He's holding his phone in front of him to show my mother what's going on.

"What were you thinking?" Dad says.

"You could've fallen and broken your head!" Mom tells me.

"Worse," Dad grumbles, "he could've broken the head of a kid who *uses* their head."

Mom sighs. "Alley just isn't a good fit with traditional education."

"On the other hand," I say, to make her feel better, "I'm *great* at Extreme Schooling."

Weirdly, this does not cheer her up.

The principal and my dad take turns scolding me. My parents are too nice to punish me, though. I've given them tips, but they never learn.

So when they're really mad, they threaten me with Grannie Blatt.

Maybe your grandmother is a sweet old lady who spoils you with all-you-can-eat pizza and Daily Cash Prizes. My *other* grandmother is like that, but Grannie Blatt is more of the "busted headphones" type: she pinches my ears and makes scary noises.

I'm pretty sure my parents are as scared of her as I am. That's why she's such a good threat.

"If you don't shape up," Mom tells me on Dad's phone, "we'll let Grannie Blatt enroll you at Steggles Academy."

I clutch my chest in horror. "Noooo!"

Before she retired, Grannie Blatt worked as a lunch lady. I usually like lunch ladies: they hand out food, not tests. What's not to like?

But my grandmother is single-handedly responsible for banning soda from every school in town. That's some pure, unsweetened evil. Also, she didn't lady her lunches in a normal human cafeteria. No, she scooped the tuna at the *other* school in town: Steggles Academy.

Steggles isn't a school so much as a factory that assembles pod-robots for the Alien Overlords. To the untrained eye, the kids there look 92 percent human . . .

but they wear uniforms. I'm talking neckties and shiny black shoes. Let's just say that *everyone* at Steggles would laugh at Bunny Boy, while Cameron Sykes would become class president.

"Your grandmother will pull some strings to get you in," Dad tells me.

"Those aren't strings," I tell him. "They're daggers. And she's not pulling them, she's stabbing them in my back!"

"And," he continues, "you'll have to stay at her apartment."

I re-clutch my chest. "What? How? *Why?*"

"Our house isn't in the right district for Steggles, Alley."

"Because we're not warp-droids from Nebula Six!"

"In order to transfer, you'll need to officially live across town," Principal Kugelmeyer tells me.

"With Grannie Blatt." Dad gives a little shudder. "But only for a few days a week."

"Your grandmother is eager to spend more time with you," Mom says, and glances nervously at Dad from the phone.

"She thinks you'd thrive in a more structured environment," Dad says, and glances back nervously at Mom on the phone.

See? They're as scared of her as I am. Still, I'll get in trouble if I mention that she's a swamp creature, so I just moan, "Not *Steggles*."

"It's an excellent school," the principal says.

"Yeah, they make the best androids in town."

"If you shape up," Mom tells me, "you can stay at Blueberry Hill. And if not . . . well, you take this school rivalry too seriously."

"We're not rivals. We're enemies."

Facts about Steggles Academy:

1) It's built on a squirrel cemetery.
2) The school color is "robotic evil."
3) The hallways smell like pickled boogers.
4) The baseball team is powered by android targeting systems.
5) The students are all artificial life-forms wearing pleated pants.

Those are the facts. And here is the proof:

    1) The Steggles Stallions crush
       the Blueberry Hill Ladybugs
       every single game.

    2) I have personally smelled the
       hallways.

    3) I spotted an UNDEAD SQUIRREL
       on their lawn while biking past.

Speaking of which, there's a rumor that some Absolute Legend from our school biked past last year, yelling, "Saint Eggles!" while hurling eggs. That's only a rumor, though.

For the next few days, my behavior is perfect. I don't sprinkle glitter in the lockers. I don't climb onto the roof. I don't steal the earthworms from eighth-grade science class.

I'm an angel.

I'm a dream.

I'm so bored that pencil sharpening is my new favorite activity.

I need to do something fun . . . but not *so* fun that I get in trouble. Luckily, I remember my Foolproof Plan: make lots of choices, so *some* of them turn out to be good.

Which is why on Tuesday, when I'm choosing between belly-surfing the fan room stairs and balancing cafeteria trays on my head, I compromise by doing both.

Here's what you need to know: the fan room isn't a room. It's a short hallway off the cafeteria, with an even shorter stairwell. It's called the fan room for two reasons:

    1) It's where the school trophy case is kept—so "fan" like "sports fan."

    2) There's a ceiling fan that never stops spinning. Nobody knows why.

The fan room is always empty, which means there's no way I'll get caught. Still, I don't take any chances: I ask my friend to watch for teachers while I catch a tray-wave.

That's Chowder. His real name is Charlie Howder, and he's carrying those weeds because he falls in love twice a month. He thinks every day is

Valentine's Day, and if you ever hear him clear his throat, RUN. He's about to recite a love poem.

"Dude," Chowder says, peering around the stairwell. "So amazing."

"I know." I groan, under the heap of cafeteria trays. "But next time I'll snowboard instead of belly-surfing."

"What?" he says.

"What-what?" I groan.

"What-what-what?" he says.

I almost groan *What-what-what-what?* because I'm not a quitter. Then I realize that he's not even looking at me.

He's gazing dopily at Maya Roman, who is standing nearby, playing with her phone.

"What rhymes with 'Maya'?" he asks me. "Other than 'Hiya'?"

I groan again, but this time not from pain. This time because I've seen that expression on his face before. He's composing a poem.

"'Papaya'!" Chowder half closes his eyes. "She's smarter than an apple, and sweeter than papaya. . . ."

"Huh?" Maya says.

"Chowder's in love with you," I tell her.

"Huh," Maya repeats, and doesn't look up from her phone.

There are two reasons for this:

One, she knows Chowder. He falls in love like rain falls in puddles.

Two, she started a game of *Realm Ruler* in fifth grade and spent the last year building a medieval queendom. She's fought wars, fed peasants, and built castles. She's one of the few kids brave enough to use her phone during school hours, because she cares more about that game

18

than anything in the real world. Including one lovesick Chowder.

"Can we sit together at lunch?" Chowder asks her.

"You'll distract me."

"I'll bring you a burrito! And I'll help with your game."

"Well, I am kind of stuck," Maya says. "A goblin horde is marching across the Forgotten Mountains."

"Which mountains?" I cleverly ask, from beneath the pile of trays.

"Why can't your army beat them?" Chowder asks, as they head toward the cafeteria.

I push a few trays away, and a piping voice says, "Ooh, fun! My turn!"

When I peer upward, the sight chills my blood.

Icicles form in my veins and penguins waddle along my spine. Because a bunch of kindergarteners are at the top of the stairs, clutching cafeteria trays. They're about to hurl themselves down.

Now, I don't know if you've ever found yourself half-buried by cafeteria trays while a mob of rug monkeys prepare to throw themselves to their doom. Maybe you have, and maybe you haven't.

It's a little . . . what's the word? Oh, right: *terrifying.* I mean, it's one thing for a sixth grader to bodysurf downstairs, but it's not safe for knee-high mini-humans.

So I spring into action.

Well, first there's a moment when, for some reason, I remember Principal Kugelmeyer saying, *The other kids copy you, the other kids copy you . . .*

Then I spring. Or, at least, I bellow, "STOP! DON'T DO THAT, YOU BUG-EYED TATER TOTS!"

The kindergarteners pause mid-hurl. The ringleader, a girl with a frizzy ponytail, squints at me. "But *you* did it."

"Aha!" I shamble to my feet. "That's where you're wrong!"

"We all saw you," she says.

"Did you?" I ask, attempting to confuse her. "Did you really?"

"Yes," she says, extremely unconfused.

"Well, well!" I rub my sore elbow. "I guess there's no telling either way."

"Here goes!" the girl says.

She's about to launch when a new voice pipes up: "Emulating Alley's uncontrolled descent strikes me as profoundly unwise."

I'm not sure what half those words mean, but I get the overall gist.

So I snap, "Don't encourage them!"

"That was not my intent," the bunny-suited kid says, and the girl steps forward.

She grips her tray like a snowboarder on a mountain peak. She's two seconds from lift-off and honestly, I'm impressed. I expect great things from this kid, if she survives kindergarten.

Which seems unlikely at the moment. So I dash up the stairs, bellowing again: "HAVE YOU EVER PLAYED BONKY ROLL?"

"Muh?" she asks, pausing.

"The game, Bonky Roll. I just invented it. Have you ever played?"

"Um, no."

I snatch a slightly chewed lunch roll from one of her friends. "Okay, everyone get ready! The goal is to keep the roll in the air, using nothing but your tray."

I toss the roll at the ringleader girl.

She whacks it with her tray, a nice high lob. She's a natural.

A second kid bonks the roll, and a third smacks it against the wall and a fourth kid misses the ricochet. Everyone groans, and they start again.

They swing, they spin, they cheer—they totally forget about tray-surfing. The fan room is not strewn with broken kindergarteners, and even better, I didn't get caught!

I pause for a moment to enjoy the happy *bonk* of bread roll against cafeteria tray, and a voice squeals, "Watch out!"

The roll is whipping toward the kid in the bunny suit. Now personally, I *like* getting pelted by a welcoming muffin or thwacked by a cheerful bun. It's a friendly way to greet a buddy.

But that Bunny Boy might not agree, so I snatch the tray from his hands and knock the roll away.

I save the kid. I save the day. I win!

Except for one teensy problem:

There was a burrito on his tray.

A burrito that launched into the air when I swung.

A burrito that smacked into the ceiling fan.

So, in other words, the burrito just hit the fan.

For an instant, the world stands still . . . then a blizzard of beans pelts me.

Three seconds later, I am more guacamole than human and the fan room looks like an explosion in a salsa factory.

And as I hunch there with shredded cheese in my hair, I hear a noise.

A sort of army chant. Getting louder. Coming closer: *"Hut, hut, hut . . ."*

It's Cameron Sykes. He marches in, looking for someone to rat on—and records me with his phone.

Principal Kugelmeyer likes me. I know that because I once heard her say, "He has the heart of a lion and the brain of a baked potato."

Lions? Awesome.

Baked potatoes? Delicious!

Also, she said, "Alley would throw himself in front of a train to save you—the *wrong* train, but still."

THE WRONG TRAIN →

THE TRAIN IN PERIL ↓

However, right now she doesn't look so friendly. She's sitting behind her desk without saying anything. Staring at me.

I squirm in my chair. I can't defend myself, because Cameron Sykes already posted the video to the school website. I had one last chance, and I blew it. My parents are going to make me spend half the week with Grannie Blatt and the *whole* week at Steggles "Androids 'R' Us" Academy.

Principal Kugelmeyer's eyes drill holes in space and time.

I open my mouth to explain—again—that I was saving those kindergarteners' lives. Then I close my mouth—again. Every time I try to explain, I just make things worse.

"I'm giving you one *final* final chance," she says.

"Yes!" I leap from my chair. "Thanks! Good talk!"

"Sit down!" she booms.

I unleap from my chair.

"Your parents," she says, "want to send you to Steggles Academy immediately."

I moan in horror.

"However," Principal Kugelmeyer says, "I asked them to hold off."

I peer at her. "You did?"

"Yes. I'm not convinced that Steggles is a good fit for you."

"It's not! Mostly because I'm an earth-based life-form."

"It's an excellent school, Alley. I used to teach there. Principal Voss is a friend. But he and I have different approaches. I support student individuality, while he . . ."

"Assembles droids?" I ask.

". . . provides a more structured environment." Principal Kugelmeyer pins me with her gaze. "If you want to stay at Blueberry Hill, you need to prove that you're serious."

I nod. "Will do."

"By getting an A on your science test next week."

"What happened to being serious? I can't get an A! Science isn't my subject."

"What *is* your subject?"

Now I'm on firmer ground. "Recess. I also excel at bathroom breaks."

"You can do this," she says. "I believe in you."

"Why?" I ask.

She peers at me blankly. There are some questions that even principals can't answer.

"How about I get a C plus?" I ask. "And we round up? "

"An *A*!"

"I've *never* gotten an A in science!"

"You'll have help this time. I signed you up for a HOST."

"Oh, great! Thanks! Perfect!" I'm hugely relieved and have only one question: "What's a host?"

"A HOST is a member of our peer mentoring program."

Except for "peer" and "mentoring," I understand every word she just said.

"Sure," I say. "That."

"Helping Other Students Thrive?" She eyes me. "HOST. We put posters in every classroom, Alley! How can you not know?"

"Knowing isn't my specialty," I say, because I don't want her to feel bad. "Like, how can six times three be eighteen? It just doesn't make any sense."

Principal Kugelmeyer rumbles. "HOST is a program that assigns advanced students to help ones who are struggling. Your HOST will keep you on track."

"On *track*," I say, with a nod of understanding.

"Alley?" the principal says.

"Hello! Good morning! Still here!"

"Just get the A," she says, "or you'll end up at Steggles."

So that's how I find myself in the multipurpose room, waiting to meet my HOST. The student volunteers are usually eighth graders, which is cool. I like hanging with older kids and they mostly like me, too.

I'm even happier when an eighth-grade girl named Swati comes in. She's awesome. She wears eye makeup and motorcycle boots.

"Hey," I say.

"Hey," she says.

This is going super well so far, so I say, "Hey, hey."

She laughs. "Are you waiting for your mentee?"

My vocabulary isn't great, but I know *exactly* what a "mentee" is:

Manatees are marine mammals sometimes known "sea-cows" or "mentees" apparently.

"Sure!" I say. "Who doesn't want to meet a sea cow?"

She laughs again. "Your *mentee*, Alley. The kid who you're helping."

"Oh! No, *I'm* the manatee! I need help with a test."

"The science test? That's you?" She squeezes my arm. "Well, your HOST will be here in a sec. He's new, but he's great."

Then she leaves and Cube comes in. "Cube" is short for QB, which is short for quarterback, but Cube isn't short for anything. He's huge, a star athlete and super-nice guy.

"Alley!" he bellows in greeting.

"Cube-y!" I reply, and we do the handshake he taught me last year.

"You're going to ace this test!" he roars.

"One hundred percent! Well, with your help."

"Oh, *I'm* not your HOST." Cube gives me a friendly slap on the back. "Your HOST is even better than me."

My vision flickers, because that's what happens when Cube thumps you. He says he'll catch me later and I grab the edge of a table, waiting for my bones to stop rattling.

"I am pleased to make your formal acquaintance," a voice says from around my kneecaps. "My name is Rexinald Wrigley, but you may call me Rex."

When my vision clears, there is a bunny standing in front of me. Carrying a briefcase.

It's that kid! That fourth grader wearing the bunny onesie! His ears are long and velvety but his eyes are sharp.

I blink at him. "Er, what?"

"I am pleased to make your formal acquaintance. My name is Rexinald Wrigley, but you may call—"

"No, I heard you! And, uh, it's good to meet you, too, li'l buddy, but I'm waiting for my HOST right now."

"I regret to say that I must disagree," the kid tells me.

"Huh?"

"You are no longer waiting for your HOST." He climbs onto the chair beside me. "For I am he."

"Hee? I thought you were Rex."

"I am your HOST." He pops open his brief-case. "Now, then. Our goal is to secure you an A on your science project."

"You're my HOST?"

"I am."

"You?" I squint at him. "Are my HOST?"

"Indeed."

"In other words," I say, "my HOST is you?"

"That is correct."

"But you're, like, seven!"

"I am, admittedly, younger than the average HOST. However, my assistance will ensure that you are not compelled to reestablish your residency in a new school district."

For a second, I almost understand what he's talking about . . . no. It's gone.

"Settle down, Captain Vocabulary," I say. "You'll *what*?"

"I shall guarantee your continued attendance at this educational establishment."

I blink. "Once more, with little words?"

"I'll help you stay at Blueberry Hill," he explains.

"By getting you an A on your science presentation."

"My science *test*."

"Ah." He pulls a page from his briefcase. "If you consult the lesson assignment, you'll discover that the student in question—"

"What question?"

His bunny ears seem to droop. "I mean *you*, Alley."

"I'm the student in question?"

"Indeed."

"Neat! What's the question?"

"Several questions begin to occur to me," he says, in a funny sort of voice. "However, my point is that you may choose between taking a test and giving a presentation."

"I can?"

"Yes. And your vivacious personality is clearly better suited to giving a presentation than taking a test. That is the key to my approach."

I don't know what "vivacious" means, and I don't care. Because an explosion just went off in my brain. A *good* explosion. A happy, toasted-marshmallow explosion.

Because when Rex said "the key," I remembered. . . .

When teachers grade tests, they use a "key," which is a sheet of paper with all the correct answers—almost like they don't know this stuff themselves.

Ever since I got to Blueberry Hill, there's been a rumor about the Golden Keys, a bunch of binders with the answers to every test in every class in every grade.

The ultimate cheat codes.

It's only a rumor, though. Or so I'd thought,

until one day last year when I stayed after school to improve some signs, like turning Cafeteria into Cafarteria.

I almost got caught by a couple of teachers. So I hid in a locker while they walked past.

"... wall chart ... special colors," one said, her voice muffled.

"Sounds good," the other said, his voice loud as a leaf blower.

"Where do we keep the Golden ... Keys?" the muffled one asked.

"The teachers' lounge," the loud one said.

"Eeeeee!" I said.

"Did you hear that?" the muffled one asked.

"Squeaky doors," the loud one said.

"Where in the lounge?" the muffled one asked.

"In the cabinet. It has one of those awful locks, but the combination is written on a poster on the wall."

"Eeeeee!" I said.

"Did you hear that?" the muffled one asked.

"A third grader's losing a tooth," the loud one said.

I waited until they left, then discovered I was jammed inside the locker like a crayon in a preschooler's nostril. No matter how I squirmed, I couldn't get out.

That's a different story, though.

Back to *this* story: I never bothered looking for the Golden Keys, because I don't like cheating. However, I like school uniforms, zombie squirrels, and plucking Grannie Blatt's chin hairs even less.

So now I need to:
1) sneak into the teachers' lounge
2) unlock the cabinet
3) find the Golden Keys
4) memorize the answers to the science test, and
5) GET AN A!

"Forget presentations," I tell Rex in the multi-purpose room. "I'm taking the test."

"I cannot endorse that approach," he says.

"Huh?"

His bunny ears point forward. "Giving a verbal report is your wisest course. A presentation will highlight your strengths."

"Fah!" I say. "My strengths are exactly what a presentation *won't* highlight."

"Why is that?"

"Oh, you want to know why, do you?"

"I do."

"Then I'll tell you. Come warm your paws by the fire, young bunny, while Uncle Alley relates

39

a story so terrifying it would give a goose people pimples. Are you ready?"

"I am."

"Cast your mind back to the Time Before. To a long-ago era, now lost in the mists of history. I was in fifth grade, and—"

"You're talking about last year?"

"Well, yeah. Last year. We had a group project in science class. My subject was the three kinds of rocks. There's, um, sedentary and ignoramus, and what's the other one?"

"Sedimentary, igneous, and metamorphic."

"Easy for you to say." I gaze across the multipurpose room. "Anyway, I was in charge of bringing in a bunch of rocks, but I forgot and we got a C."

Rex waits for me to continue, but I don't. I just keep gazing.

"Is that . . . the whole story?" he asks.

"Pretty much," I say, and don't tell him that I tried to improvise.

Everyone thought I was kidding . . .

Except for my partners.

Who got Cs.

Because of me.

"So I'm definitely taking the test," I tell Rex. "I'll ace it for sure."

"Have you ever 'aced' a science test in the past?"

"Well, not exactly."

"Why is this test different from all other tests?" Rex asks.

I answer in a flash, trained by years of Passover seders, "Because on all other tests we don't dip our vegetables even once, but on this test we dip twice!"

"I fail to see the relevance of vegetables, dipped or otherwise," Rex says.

"Oh, right!" This isn't a Passover seder. "Er, because I know this topic cold."

"What *is* the topic?"

My mind blanks. "Well, science. The science of scientific . . . science."

"The water cycle," Rex prompts.

"Right! Of course! I knew that."

"Did you?" he says.

"Yes! I am an expert on the water cycle. *You* probably think it's an ocean-based motorbike!"

"I beg your pardon?" he says.

"Water," I say. "Cycle. Listen up, young bunny, as I drop seventeen pounds of wisdom on your cottontail. You cannot *ride* a water cycle!"

"I am aware," Rex says, "that the water cycle is not a vehicle."

"I learned that the hard way," I admit. "After I drew a picture of a TideStomper Aquacycle and got a zero."

"What is a TideStomper Aquacycle?" Rex asks.

"Imagine a Jet Ski with water cannons—and in the background a Killclass Seven spaceship is battling a gigantic frombie."

He blinks at me. "Pardon?"

"A frombie. A frog-zombie. But gigantic."

Rex gazes at me, awed by my genius.

"And now you want to take the test?" he finally asks.

"I'm going to crush it," I tell him. "Like a wrecking ball in an eggshell museum."

Despite the seventeen pounds of knowledge, Rex *still* thinks I should do a presentation. You just can't reason with rabbits. He's a sweet little dude, but he doesn't know my golden secret. So I keep refusing to work with him until he says goodbye.

Except instead of saying "goodbye," he says, "Then I shall bid you adieu."

"I shall *raise* you a dew!" I tell him, and leave without a HOST.

That's okay. I don't need his help.

I do need *someone's* help, though. Someone to act as a lookout when I break into the teachers' lounge.

After my next class, I tug Maya down the hallway. "Come on!"

"Where to?" she asks.

"Teachers' lounge. I need to sneak in. You're my lookout."

Maya frowns. "Why would I do that?"

"It'll be like a mission in your game."

"Ooh. You're *raiding* the teachers' lounge!"

"Yeah."

She stands a little taller. "You're invading enemy territory!"

"Well, I wouldn't call them 'enemies' . . ."

"Are you trying to steal something?"

"No!" I'm only trying to memorize a few answers. "I just need to find the Golden—"

"Gold!" Maya's eyes blaze. "That's *awesome*! I love a raid. Dodging ogre sentries, climbing castle walls! On my raids, I always use snake soldiers and cast a Spell of Befuddlement."

"Uh, Maya? This is happening in the real world."

She sighs. "So no snake soldiers."

"Or fuddlement."

"*Be*fuddlement."

"I don't care what grade it got!" I drag her around the corner. "I just need a lookout!"

"Right now? We can't! We have PE in five minutes. And also—"

"We'll cut class."

"And *also*," she repeats, "look!"

I peer past her, expecting the hallway will be (a) quiet, (b) empty, and (c) safe. Instead, it is (d) none of the above. Teachers are bumbling around like fruit flies on rotten bananas . . . because someone brought *cupcakes*.

And Rule One is, never get between a teacher and a chocolate treat.

Maya drags me to gym class, and I spend the rest of the day waiting for another chance to raid the teachers' lounge. School keeps interrupting, though. Honestly, I'd get way more done without all these classes.

When the final bell rings, I head outside and pretend to wait for a bus. I'll sneak away in a minute and have the lounge to myself. I mean, not even *teachers* will stay after school for stale cupcakes. Will they?

"Alexander!" a dread voice calls.

The breeze stops blowing.

The sun stops shining.

The water stops cycling.

"Alexander!" Grannie Blatt repeats, from

outside my dad's car. "I hope you're wearing deodorant!"

What happens next is, a fiery chasm doesn't appear in the sidewalk and swallow me whole. Because sometimes wishes don't come true.

"Hi, Grannie," I say, trudging closer.

"Because you're at the age when boys start to stink," Grannie explains, so loudly that a flock of crows scatters in the next town.

My father gives me a sympathetic look from the driver's seat. I slip into the car before Grannie Blatt starts yelling about how she potty trained me.

"Why don't you spend the night with your grandmother?" my father asks me. "As a sort of test?"

Except he's not really asking me, he's telling me. Grannie Blatt must've bullied him into agreeing.

"As a special treat," Grannie Blatt says, squeezing into the back seat beside me, "I even have your favorite."

Now that is a surprise. "Really? You got *Premeditated Vehicular Assault 3*?"

"What? What are you saying? What is that?"

"It's a video game."

"Feh! Such a waste of time! No, I made calf's-foot jelly. Your favorite."

Why would she think that? I'd rather eat a dozen glue sticks than one spoonful of calf's-foot jelly.

Still, I politely say, "Gee, thanks."

"Anything for my third-favorite grandson." She licks her thumb, then scrubs at my cheek. "It would kill you to splash water on your face? Look at all these children!"

REALITY

GRANNIE-VISION

"Dressed like ragamuffins," Grannie Blatt scoffs. "At Steggles, the children are always clean and tidy."

"And mechanical," I say.

"Don't mumble!" She blows her nose into a handkerchief with a *HONK*. "And your grades are worse than those rags you're wearing. Well, a few hours of homework every night will fix that."

Enough with being polite! I open my mouth to demand what, exactly, is wrong with the rags I'm wearing . . . and she wipes my cheek with her snotty handkerchief.

I close my mouth. The car flickers around me. A grandmother capable of doing *that* is a grandmother capable of doing anything.

"—and they'll let you enroll in Steggles as a favor to me," she's saying, when the car stops flickering. "As long as you live with me half the week. Oh, we're home."

Except we're not at *my* home. We're at hers.

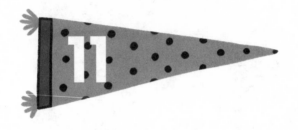

That is the Shrieking Horror that awaits me if I don't get an A on my test: three nights a week with used handkerchiefs, and five days a week with soulless kidroids.

I spend the next morning thinking about that. Worrying about it. Trying not to *cry* about it. Which is no fun, so here's a picture of an intergalactic giraffe fighting a robotic butt.

When I trudge past the gym, Rex is sitting in the hallway, looking about as cheerful as I feel. His ears are drooping, his head is bowed.

So I plop down beside him and say, "Hey, Rex."

"Greetings, Alley," he says.

"What's up?"

He sighs. "To my shame, I've been instructed to remain here for the duration of my physical education class."

"You got sent to sit in the hall, huh?"

"That is precisely the case." He lowers his voice. "And I am concerned about incurring a blemish on my permanent record."

After I run that through my Rex-to-English dictionary, I'm pretty sure he means that he's scared of getting in trouble. So I tell him, "Nah, they won't even call your parents the first few times, unless you did something really . . . what's that word? Ingenious?"

"Egregious?"

"That too," I agree. "Like if you accidentally drew goofy faces on all the basketballs with a permanent marker."

A smile quivers on the edge of his mouth. "'Accidentally?'"

"Yeah, I only meant to do the dodgeballs, but I got carried away."

"Which could happen to anyone," he says, his ears perking slightly.

"Exactly!" I squint at him. "So why are you in trouble?"

"On account of repeated dress code violations."

"Huh?"

"I am not comfortable wearing gym clothes."

"Oh! Yeah, you're not a big fan of shorts and T-shirts, are you?"

"Regretfully not. The teacher requested that I wear my 'gym kit,' but . . ."

"But what? What'd you say?"

"That I prefer not to change."

I laugh. "Right on, you legend. Never change."

He starts to say something, then stops. Then we just sit there quietly, together, listening to the squeak of sneakers from the gym.

I can tell he feels better, though, after a minute or two.

And, for some reason, so do I.

By lunchtime, I'm ready to get back to work. Not to *school*work, obviously. To *sneak*work.

So I corner Maya in the cafeteria. "Are you ready to be lookout?"

"If you're not stealing gold," she asks, "why are you raiding the teachers' lounge?"

"Because I don't want to spend my days in a robot factory and my nights rubbing lotion on an old lady's feet."

"Zounds!" Maya says, which she got from her game. "Let's go!"

Two minutes later, I'm peering around a corner toward the lounge. It's quiet and still, like a haunted house on a sunny summer day. Still, there's no telling when a fright of teachers will appear, rattling their chains at the coffeemaker and moaning at the fridge.

"Warn me if you see anyone," I tell Maya. "Stay quiet and—"

"Hey!" Chowder yells, galumphing closer. "What're we doing?"

"Staying quiet!" I whisper.

"What're we doing that for?" he roars.

"I'm on lookout for Alley," Maya tells him.

Chowder squints at her. "Um, he's right there."

"No, I'm watching for *teachers*."

"Oh! I'll help," Chowder says. "They're easy to spot."

"Fine," I say. "If anyone comes, yell something."

"Like what?" Maya asks.

"Something no teacher would ever say." I think

for a second. "'Badger butts!' or 'Who farted?' or 'My nose is full of boogers.'"

"Sure," Maya says, swiping at her phone.

Chowder squints at the screen. "Are those the goblins?"

"Yeah, they're almost across the Forgotten Mountains."

"Which mountains?" I ask, quick as a flash.

Then I slip away.

I tiptoe around the corner and sneak down the hall.

I camouflage myself against the bulletin board.

I wait for the perfect moment, then dive, roll, and leap into the teachers' lounge.

I expect to find comfy couches, a hot tub, and a popcorn machine. Instead, the room looks like the leftovers of other classrooms.

At least it's empty.

Still, I listen with all my ears for "badger butts" or "booger nose." In fact, there's a chant inside my head: *badger butts who farted boogers, badger butts who farted boogers* . . . If I hear any of those words, I'll scramble out the door and sprint away.

To my left, there is the Saddest Couch in America. It's gray and saggy. It looks like the place where cushions go to die.

To my right, there's a cafeteria table with a GRATEST TEECHER EVAR mug. Which is a little boastful, if you ask me.

And directly across from me, tucked into exactly the right place, there is a complete lack of cabinets. I'm not even talking *zero* cabinets. There are *negative* cabinets against that wall.

The teachers' lounge whirls around me like a hammock in a hurricane. I grab a chair to steady myself, gaping with horror at the Wall of Cabinetlessness.

And that's when I spot a rectangular shape on the wall. A cabinet-shaped shape. A place where the cabinet *used* to be.

They moved it.

Which means the cabinet is still *somewhere*— and I still need the combination. I will find this cabinet. I will unearth the Golden Keys. I will achieve a test score never before seen at Blueberry Hill—or, at least, an A-minus-minus.

I scramble along the wall, peering at posters until I stop at one showing a kitten hanging from a branch. There, in the corner, is a four-digit number: 5-4-3-2.

"Yes!" I punch the air, then recite the number aloud so I'll remember: "Five-four-three-two-one."

Perfect! I'm halfway to the door before I realize something isn't right.

I turn back. 5-4-3-2. Very tricky, leaving off the *1* like that, but I've got it now. Five-four—

A teacher opens the door.

My eyeballs explode and my lungs catch fire. I'm caught! I'm trapped! There's nowhere to run, no time to hide.

So I cleverly launch plan B, which is "Freeze and Tremble."

Except the teacher doesn't come inside. He doesn't even look inside. He stays in the doorway, talking to someone in the hall.

Most kids, at this point, would stick with plan B. After all, it's working perfectly so far.

Not me! I burst into action, and a second later I'm sliding beneath the table.

Safe!

Well, actually . . . *trapped*! But at least I'm out of sight.

The teacher comes inside. Then another teacher, and another and another. Talking to one another. Pouring coffee. Sitting at the chairs around *my* table.

And listen, I like teachers. I've always been a fan. Still, you don't want to be surrounded by their knees. Trust me on this. It's not a pretty sight.

I don't make a sound. I barely breathe. Okay, new plan: hide until the next class starts, then run for it.

Except just then one of the chairs scrapes the floor, making a *BRRRRRAP* sound.

And a teacher says—I am not even kidding—"Who farted?"

Seriously, who *hires* these people?

That's not the big problem, though. The big

problem is that I've been listening so hard for "who farted" that I lose my mind. The instant I hear the words, I scramble from under the table and race for the door.

In full view of all the teachers.

Including Ms. Vergara, the PE teacher, who grabs my arm.

13

"Alley!" Ms. Vergara barks. "What on earth were you doing under the table?"

"Guh, um," I explain. "Ha ha!"

"You are in serious trouble, young man."

"Well, the thing is," I say. "What the thing is, is—"

A knock sounds at the open door.

"Yes, Rex?" one of the teachers asks. "Can we help you?"

"Alley found it!" Rex announces, reaching out to take my hands.

So I let him, because I am polite. Other things I am: stunned and terrified.

"What is going on here?" Ms. Vergara demands.

"I'm sorry for the trouble," Rex tells her, one bunny ear flopping down apologetically. "Someone threw my asthma inhaler into the lounge. I was fearful of entering, so Alley did so in my place."

A silence falls.

I hold my breath.

The entire school teeters on a seesaw.

"It must have slid under the table," Rex says, and shows them the inhaler he's holding.

It looks like he just took it from me. Like I found it under the table and gave it to him. It's so convincing that even *I* think that's what happened.

"Oh, Alley!" a teacher gushes. "Well done."

"Now *that* is a good choice," another teacher says.

Ms. Vergara says, "He has the intellectual

capacity of a chicken nugget, but he always sticks up for younger kids."

I would thank her, because everyone knows that chicken is the smartest of the nuggets, but I'm too busy gazing at Rex in awe. How did he *do* that? This kid is magic. He's a unicorn. I don't know why a unicorn is wearing a bunny suit, but no doubt he has his reasons.

I'm stunned and smiling as the teachers' praise wafts me from the lounge. Well, plus Rex tugs me into the hallway with his paw.

When the door closes, I turn to him. "You legend! You velveteen dream bunny! Why didn't you *tell* me you're a tiny genius? Thank you!"

"I am happy to oblige," he says.

"I'm also happy with that word you just said!"

"Oblige?"

"That's the one. I'm happy with a blige, I'm happy with *two* bliges. The only thing I'm *not* happy with is . . ."

I spring around the corner to yell at Maya and Chowder, the worst lookouts in the world, but they're not there.

"Oh," I say. "Those dorkfish."

"I believe they were distracted by Maya's game," Rex says. "In their defense, defeating the goblin horde in the Forgotten Mountains is quite difficult."

"Which mountains?" I ask, in my clever way.

"Very witty," Rex says.

"I know! Thank you! Because they're *Forgotten* Mountains, so—" I squint at him. "Wait a second. You play *Realm Ruler*?"

"No longer. I ruled all the realms after two weeks. Have you reconsidered my proposal?"

"Yes and no," I say. "Depending on what that means."

"Will you let me help you prepare a presentation?" he asks. "For science class. To earn the A. Instead of taking the test."

"Oh! Nah, not after I've come so far."

When Rex raises himself to his full height, the tips of his bunny ears almost reach my chin. "Come how far? What progress have you made?"

"Five-four-three-two," I announce.

"I beg your pardon?"

"*You* probably think there's a 'one' at the end! But they cannot fool me."

"What significance does that sequence hold?" he asks, still tugging me down the hallway. "Er. What does it mean?"

"It's the combination to the Golden Keys," I say, and tell him everything. "So now I just need to find where they moved that cabinet."

Rex frowns. "I am not convinced that the Golden Keys will aid your—"

"Shhh!" I tell him. "Don't jinx me."

"No jinx intended. I am merely concerned that—"

"Shut your whiskers!"

"I feel I must say—"

"Hushbunny!"

He sighs. "Very well. You are certain I cannot change your mind?"

"Absolutely."

"In that case, the cabinet you are seeking is locked in a supply closet on the third floor."

See? An absolute unicorn.

Here's my new plan:

    1) Cut English class.

    2) Sneak to the third floor.

    3) Pick the supply closet lock. (The internet has a tutorial for *everything*.)

    4) Slip inside, 5-4-3-2 the cabinet, grab the Golden Keys, and STAY AT MY OWN SCHOOL.

Another flawless plan! Except the first step is *Cut English*, and somehow, when Rex stops talking, I'm already standing outside my classroom.

And Mr. Kapowski is looming near the door.

No problem. He hasn't seen me yet, so I blend into a nearby mural like an elf wearing a Cloak of Invisibility.

Unfortunately, Mr. Kapowski is like a gnome wearing a Bow Tie of Spotting Students, and drags me to my desk.

"What is going on with you?" Chowder whispers.

"You mean other than getting shipped to Steggles Manufacturing and spending half my life at my grandmother's house?"

"Oh! I forgot about that."

"How could you forget?"

"I've been thinking about Maya's eyebrows.

Also, what's so bad about your grandmother?"

"Used handkerchiefs, yellow toenails—" I sputter, before blurting, "She'll make me eat calf's-foot jelly!"

"What even is that?" he asks.

I take a breath. "You know how fish fingers aren't actually fingers, and string cheese isn't actually string?"

"Sure."

"Well, calf's-foot jelly *is* actually jelly made from calves' feet."

He shudders. "Like grape jelly? But from hooves?"

"Like *garlic* jelly," I tell him. "But from hooves."

We fall silent, pondering the horror. At least I *think* that's what we're pondering. Except then Chowder says, "I wonder if Maya will let me walk home with her."

"She rides the bus," I remind him.

He sighs dippily. "She's the *best* at riding the bus."

"You're a dorkfish," I say.

"You're a corncob," he says.

"You're both disruptions," Mr. Kapowski says, and scolds us for whispering.

I feel bad, because Mr. Kapowski always tries to make class fun. And I feel even worse, because I ruined everything for him once.

He'd been talking about an ancient Greek dude who wrote books that were mostly people talking. Mr. Kapow said that was a good way to teach, through conversations.

Which was true! The only problem was, I'd been having a conversation of my own at the time, and totally ignoring his lesson.

That's probably why he'd called on me. "Alley? Please tell the class your favorite thing about Play-Doh."

I wasn't sure why he'd asked such an easy question. Still, I immediately said, "The smell! Plus, I like rolling Play-Doh into worms and—"

The entire class started laughing. Not just laughing, *howling*.

Because it turned out that the old Greek dude was named "Plato."

That's what Mr. Kapow had said, not "Play-Doh." So I'd just announced that I loved how the ancient guy smelled and wanted to roll him into worms.

The other kids treated me like a hero, but I felt bad. Mr. Kapow had just wanted to share a cool idea and I'd messed it up. He hadn't even sent me to the principal's office. He'd just looked sad.

Ever since then, I've tried to do better. Mr. Kapow loves class participation, so today, when he starts a discussion, I join in to make him feel better.

The topic is Why Kids Don't Read More.

Mr. Kapow: *What do you like in a book?*

Me: *Rocket launchers! Barfing! Mutant frogs!*

Mr. Kapow: *Perhaps stories about your challenges and triumphs? Your personal struggles?*

Me: *I'd personally struggle to hold one of those video-game guns the size of a porta-potty.*

Mr. Kapow: *Anyone* else?

Me: *The truck that sucks sewage out of porta-potties is called a "honey wagon."*

Mr. Kapow: *In summary, there's no telling why kids don't read more.*

Here's my *new* new plan. I'll miss the bus after school. Then, while I wait for Dad, I'll raid the third-floor storage closet. Grab the Golden Keys.

Today is Friday, so I'll have all weekend to memorize the keys. Then on Monday, I'll ace the test.

The first step goes perfectly: I miss the bus.

"I need to study for a test," I tell the yard monitor. "Can I go to the library?"

The yard monitor laughs. "You! Study! A test!"

"I can verify Alley's assertion," Rex says, rabbiting beside me.

The yard monitor blinks. "Huh?"

"As Alley's HOST," Rex says, "I am in a position to corroborate his intention to apply himself to preparing for his upcoming science test."

The yard monitor is rocked by those syllables, but stays on his feet like a champ. "Oh, um. Sure. Go ahead."

After we slink inside, I grin at Rex. "We're not actually going to the library."

"I am aware that your intentions are focused elsewhere."

"We're going to the third floor!"

"Yes, I suspected you might—"

"Didn't see that coming, did you?" I pat him on the back. "Stick with me, squirt, you'll learn a few things."

"I shall stick with you," he says, "to prepare you for the presentation."

"I don't need to study! I just need the Golden Keys."

"Repeat after me," he says, and starts spouting facts about the water cycle.

I almost tell him to go away, but (a) that's mean, (b) I owe him for the teachers' lounge, and (c) he's not getting in my way or anything. He's just tagging along as I head for the stairs.

"'Cold air,'" I repeat. "'Water molecules. The sun heats the oceans.'"

He jabbers more nouns and verbs and, for all I know, adjectives.

"'The evaporative phase,'" I repeat. "'Condensation.'"

"Runoff," he says.

"'Runoff!'" I play an air-guitar solo. "*Weeyow!* Smackdown monsoon storm cycle!"

Rex clears his throat. "Percolation."

"'Perco—'" I stop short. "Jell-O!"

That last word isn't a repeat, it's a heartfelt expression of joy. Because the third-grade Hill Build Contest must've happened today. A bunch of models are displayed in the lobby near the stairway.

Most of them are neat and normal:

But one is different.
What kind of bone-
headed baby goblins built
a model out of *Jell-O*?

That's a terrible plan. It's a complete fumble. It's a massive fail.

They're my heroes. They brought twenty pounds of blueberry-flavored slime into school! Pure genius. And now it's sitting here in the lobby.

Well, not "sitting" so much as "wobbling." And I'm wobbling too—with excitement. Because an awesome new choice just appeared before me.

"I cannot support your inclination," Rex says, "to tamper with that whiffle waffle gorgonzola . . ."

Well, I don't know what he says exactly, because I'm too busy gazing at the Jell-O that is glistening before me. And, I mean, I'm only waiting around for Dad, right? It's not like I have anything else to do.

Plus, there's always time to sculpt a robotic JELL-O-butt.

The PA system says: "Alley Katz, your grand-mother is waiting in the driveway."

My heart shrivels like ~~my fingertips after a five-hour bath~~.

My heart shrivels like ~~the apple I forgot in my backpack all summer~~.

My heart shrivels like ~~a slug in a bowl of potato chips~~.

My heart just shrivels, okay? I mean, Grannie Blatt? *Again?* What happened to *this is just a test*?

"Oh no," I moan.

"You are fretful because you failed to locate the Golden Keys," Rex tells me. "However—"

"That's not why I'm full of fret!"

"Then what is the cause of your distress?"

"My grandmother! She'll chain me to her kitchen table all weekend and make me *study*."

"How unfortunate," he says, with an odd tone in his voice. "Still, perhaps that will improve your grade?"

"But at what cost, young Rex?" I ask gravely. "At what cost?"

He blinks at me. "Beg pardon?"

"The Blatt is a grandmother without mercy," I tell him. "She carries a picture of me in her purse."

"That is neither unpleasant nor unusual."

I laugh bitterly. "It shows me as a three-year-old, sitting on a potty with Cheetos in my ears."

"I retract my previous statement," he says.

"And she flashes it around like a pop-up ad! She showed my whole fourth-grade class. Plus, the only soda in her fridge is celery-flavored."

Before Rex bursts into sympathetic tears, there is a screeching from the front of the school. It sounds like a squeaky door hitting a cat's tail. Also like tires squealing when a terrible driver jerks forward and slams the brakes, then jerks forward and slams the brakes again.

My heart soars. That's the sound of Bubbie's pickup truck!

Bubbie is my *other* grandmother. My sweet and cheerful grandmother. Actually, Grannie Blatt says I'm just like Bubbie. She calls me "a chip off the old blockhead."

So I bid Rex "a dew," which makes his ears quiver happily, and race outside.

Sure enough, there's a dented old pickup truck waiting on the sidewalk. Well, *half* on the sidewalk. Bubbie never gets all four wheels on the same surface.

The passenger door creaks open and Bubbie calls, "Climb in!"

"Hi, Bubbie," I say, fastening my seat belt.

"Let me look at you!"

REALITY

BUBBIE-VISION

"My handsome *bubbeleh*!" Bubbie stomps on the gas. "So? How was your day?"

"Well, I—"

"Enough about you!" She spins the wheel wildly, scattering cars like a toddler chasing pigeons. "Let's talk about me!"

I brace against the dashboard. "How are you?"

"With my new titanium knees? I'm as strong as one of your killer robots."

"Like a Terminator!"

"Nu?" she says. "Which one is that?"

"The ones that come from the future to change the past."

"That's me in a nutshell," Bubbie says, honking the truck horn happily. "Except I came from the past to kvetch about the present."

I laugh. "Oh! That reminds me, I have a science test Monday."

"How does that remind you?"

"Well, mostly because of the kvetching."

"Kvetching" means "complaining," and the thing I want second most in the world right now is to complain to Bubbie about how unfair school is. But what I want *first* most is to ask her to help me get the A in science.

Except before I mention it, she says, "Test, shmest. There's french fries in the glove compartment."

I don't ask why there are french fries in the glove compartment. I just open the glove compartment and *ta da*! French fries. Which immediately leap to the top of the Things I Want Most in the World Right Now list, making me forget about the test and the Golden Keys—and even the kvetching.

"Help yourself," Bubbie says as the truck squeals around a corner. "Put on your hat and coat—and where's that fake beard?"

"No idea," I mumble, around a mouthful of fries.

She blasts through a yellow light. "Then strap in, Alley-gator! We're heading for the belly of the beast!"

Bubbie lives in a seniors-only place across town. They don't allow kids, so when I visit, I have to dress as an old man, in weird hats and patchy jackets and a fake beard.

I still look like a kid, of course, but nobody cares. Either that or they're afraid that if they complain, Bubbie will take revenge, like smearing hot sauce on their dentures.

When Bubbie first moved in, this what I imagined:

I also imagined *wisdom*. I mean, if you're older than rust, you should be full of knowledge and dignity, right?

Except this is what it actually looks like:

Bubbie is my favorite person. She makes everything fun. And once I tell her about the Golden Keys, she won't scold me: she'll just think of a way to help.

I open my mouth to explain, and Mr. Morris says, "Does anyone want soda?"

"Oh!" I say. "Yes, please."

"Which flavor?" he asks, showing me two bottles. "Pickle or pastrami?"

Mr. Morris once told me a story about growing up in New York City. The only telephone on his entire block was at the candy store. Any kid lucky enough to answer would get a penny for running to the apartment that was getting the call. So I asked him what kind of candy they had back in the Stone Age, and he said, "Brontosaurus Swirl," and we still make up funny flavors.

"Oh no," I say. "You're out of Broccoli Crunch *again*?"

We both laugh, he pours me a glass of cherry cola, and a lady I don't know tells me, "Mr. Morris is a member of the Greatest Generation."

I think she's kidding, so I say, "According to him!"

Except apparently that's what his generation is called: the Greatest Generation. Seriously, look it up. I mean, there's Boomers, Xers, Millennials, Z, and . . . Greatest?

That's pretty bigheaded, if you ask me. I don't say anything, though.

And I don't need to, because Bubbie says, "Greatest Generation, my wobbly bottom."

"They won World War II," the other lady sniffs.

"They were children," Bubbie says. "Do you know what they called sleeping bags in the army? 'Fart sacks.'"

"No way!" I say.

Bubbie nods. "And one night, on the boat to Germany, the soldier next to my father suddenly screamed, 'Gas attack!' Everyone woke up, scrambling for their gas masks—but guess what actually happened?"

"What?" I ask.

"Your great-grandfather farted."

The other lady clucks about showing some respect, but Bubbie doesn't care. That's one of the things I love about her. She once told me, *It's always okay to question things, Alley-gator, especially things that nobody else questions. Especially those things.*

"I never saw anything like that . . . ," Mr. Morris tells Bubbie, stroking his beard thoughtfully.

"Ha!" the other lady says.

". . . but we used to stick our butts out of moving trains to poop."

So what I'm saying is, I forget to tell Bubbie about my school problems right then.

And after the poker game, we join Zayde—my grandfather—at their apartment for a traditional Shabbos dinner. Well, traditional for *us*. We light candles, drink grape juice, and stuff ourselves on the homemade pineapple-garlic pizza that Zayde cooked.

I sleep over that night, but what with one thing and another, the Golden Keys totally slip my mind.

On Sunday, Grannie Blatt comes to our house to light a yahrzeit candle for her father. A yahrzeit candle burns for twenty-four hours straight. You light one every year, as a memorial for someone you lost, on the anniversary of their death.

Grannie Blatt says a prayer, then talks about her father a little.

She sounds sad, but *he* sounds like he kicked butt.

First he traveled to Spain to fight the fascists in the 1930s. I'm not really clear on the history, but I guess the "fascists" were Nazis before Nazis were Nazis? Anyway, he got captured and locked up in a prisoner-of-war camp for a year.

But that didn't stop him—because he kicked butt.

So after that war, he signed up to fight in World War II. He was a motorcycle messenger. He died when his bike hit a land mine.

"He fought his whole life against injustice," Dad says.

"He never backed down," Mom says.

"He was brave and kind," Grannie Blatt says. "But he was reckless, too. He never even got to meet his daughter."

"You mean you?" I ask.

"Yes, Alley. I mean me."

"Oh. That's sad."

"My father was a good man, but nobody taught him to think about the consequences." Grannie

Blatt peers at me. "Now who does *that* remind you of?"

I almost say *Captain America*, based on fighting in World War II, but Cap thinks about consequences. Then I almost say *Wolverine*, because he's more reckless, except that's not right either. So finally, I almost say *Blue Beetle*, because he's so cool. But he's DC, and I'm pretty sure that Grannie Blatt is only talking about the Marvel Universe, except now I can't even remember the question.

So I dig deep. I mean, *really* deep. Sure I forgot the question, but that doesn't mean I don't know any answers.

And the answer I say is this: "The oceans contain ninety-six percent of the earth's water."

Not bad, right? It looks like Rex's science facts are rubbing off on me! I'm pretty proud of myself, but for some reason Grannie Blatt only sighs.

At school on Monday, the clock in gym class makes rude gestures at me with its minute hand.

I'm out of time.

The test is *today*. I need to free the Golden Keys from a locked cabinet in a storage room on the third floor or I'm doomed to a life of wart-trimming and squirrel cemeteries.

My first class is gym. Which is usually nice. I'm a big fan of throwing and catching. Not to mention running, dodging, tackling, and whooping.

On the other hand, I'm not great at rules. I'm more into *dis*organized sports.

That's why Ms. Vergara isn't surprised when my warm-up involves chatting quietly with Chowder and Maya in the corner.

"What happened on Friday?" I ask.

"We were fighting goblins!" Maya says.

"*We,*" Chowder repeats, smiling at her dippily.

"I mean," I snap, "about being lookouts!"

"Oh," Maya says. "Nothing happened, did it?"

I grit every individual tooth. "Nothing but a hundred teachers coming and sitting on my head! Luckily, Rex saved me."

"Rex is great!" Maya says. "I owe him huge. He showed me how to defeat the goblin horde."

"One must alternate fireballs and ice blasts," Rex says, suddenly behind me.

I leap like a bullfrog sitting on a thumbtack. "Don't creep up on me like that!"

"Why aren't you in class?" Chowder asks him.

"A HOST is granted certain privileges. We are offered amenities such as hall passes."

The word "amenities" hits Chowder like a

cinder block during a pillow fight. He staggers, so I jump into the ring.

"Except you're not a HOST, are you?" I ask Rex. "Not without a student to help."

"I remain committed to helping *you*, Alley."

"But you still want me to give a presentation! All I want is help getting the Golden Keys."

"I shall do whatever is necessary to secure you an A. You wish to open the supply closet on the third floor?"

"Yeah. But how?"

"If you clog a nearby water fountain, it will overflow onto the floor."

"That's what clogging does," I agree.

"The water will seep into the closet," Rex says. "Then a teacher will unlock the door to dry the floor inside."

"Ooh," Chowder says. "Alley can walk right in!"

"Not alone," Rex tells him. "You and Maya must join him."

"No way! Clogging water fountains is serious trouble."

"I am confident you will face no official sanction."

"Muh?" Chowder asks.

"He means you won't get in trouble," I explain, because I'm starting to understand Rex even when he uses made-up words.

"I don't know," Maya says. "Messing with the plumbing is a big deal."

"As big a 'deal' as defeating the goblin horde?" Rex asks.

"Not even close! And I owe you for that, so . . ." She takes a breath. "Okay, I'm in."

"Me too!" Chowder announces, gazing puppy-doggily at Maya. "Clogs away!"

"Except why will a teacher let us into a wet supply closet?" she asks Rex.

"Good question," I say.

"Very good," Rex says, and looks at the mops leaning against the custodian's room.

"So what's the answer?" I ask him.

"What reason could there be," Rex asks, gesturing to the mops, "to enter a room while water is on the floor?"

"You're answering a question with another question," Chowder tells him.

"We need you to answer with an answer," I explain.

"Maybe there *is* no answer," Maya says, heaving a sigh.

"Use the mops!" Rex drums his fingers impatiently on his briefcase. "Surely the strategy is obvious."

I look at the mops.

Maya looks at the mops.

Chowder looks at the mops.

"Nope," I say. "No idea what you're talking about."

"Complete blank," Chowder reports.

"You mean use them like swords?" Maya smiles fiercely. "We'll ambush the teachers and drive them from our realm!"

Chowder salutes Maya. "At your command, milady!"

"No, no!" Rex bleats. "Just offer to mop the floor! The teacher will let you inside to clean up."

"Oh," Maya says. "That works too."

"Precisely so," Rex says.

I gaze at him in awe. This is the smartest thing

I've ever heard. "You are the kingpin of bunnies! Other rabbits nibble and hop, but you *roar*."

"Thank you," he says, giving a little bow.

"Let's grab the mops now," I tell Chowder, "then during Quiet Study we'll head upstairs."

So we edge toward the mops and—

"Alley!" Ms. Vergara bellows. "What on earth are you doing?"

"Scrub-ercising!" I wave my mop overhead. "Now swab and turn, and swab and wring!"

"Put that down and start running laps. All three of you! Give me a full mile."

I stare at her in shock and horror. A mile? A full mile? We normally only do that twice a year!

Ms. Vergara peers at Rex. "And what are *you* doing here, young man?"

"I am here," he tells her, "pursuant to my duties as an associate of the HOST program."

For a second, Ms. Vergara looks like a basketball just rebounded off her left eyebrow. Then she blinks and says, "Ah, okay."

What Rex does next is so amazing that you should take your hat off—because your brain's about to explode. He pours all his XP into Flopsy Mind Control and asks Ms. Vergara, "May I borrow these? I'll return them to the custodian when I'm finished."

"Sure," Ms. Vergara says.

"I shall place them in the stairwell for your later retrieval," Rex murmurs to me.

"Cool!" I say.

A little too loudly, because Ms. Vergara turns to me and bellows, "WHY AREN'T YOU RUN-NING? Alley, Maya, Charles!"

So we start running.

Then we keep running.

And running and running and running.

Sweat stings my eyes. My vision blurs. I run until my hair is a dripping sponge and my legs are overcooked noodles. Finally, after two and a half eternities, we finish and collapse to the floor.

Nobody moves, nobody talks. We just lie there, gasping. We are a steaming pile of sixth graders, but at least I'm totally sure that Rex moved the mops into position. Only a couple more classes, then we strike.

Except I realize during my next class that I'm *not* totally sure that Rex moved the mops into position. So I squirm until I get a bathroom pass, and then I head for the library.

I happen to know that Rex is there right now, because I keep tabs on the library.

There are two reasons for this:

One, my favorite bathroom is there, tucked away behind the reference section.

And two, Ms. Z is there. She's the librarian. She has spiky purple hair and knits creepy stuffed animals. In other words, she's awesome.

I worry about her, though. Sometimes she forgets whose side she's on. Last year, when a teacher told me to read "real" books instead of comics, Ms. Z smiled like a velociraptor and brought me a hundred graphic novels from her own collection.

So I'm always happy to see her—and at first I'm happy to see Rex, too. He's sitting at a table with a bunch of other fourth graders, and they're all chatting. Which is nice. I've never seen Rex talking to kids in his own grade before.

Then I hear what they're saying.

"Just get a backpack like everyone else," one kid tells Rex. "What's wrong with you?"

"Who carries a *briefcase*?" another kid scoffs.

Rex hunches his shoulders. "Briefcases are commonly employed by lawyers, businesspeople, and—"

"What's in there, anyway?" a third kid demands.

"I fail to comprehend," Rex says, "why the contents of my briefcase are any concern of yours."

"Yeah, what's in there?" the first kid asks. "Show us, show us!"

I pause for a second, because I'm curious about the briefcase too. My best guess is that Rex is carrying around blueprints of the school— or carrots. Or an ant colony. Or a 3D printer. Or a shrink ray. Well, I don't know; that's why I wait to see if Rex pops the lid.

But then the second kid says, "Briefcases are stupid."

Between you and me, he's not wrong. After all, what's the smartest thing a briefcase ever did? As far as I can tell, they're not nearly as clever as wheelie suitcases or sandwich bags.

Still, while you might've missed the tone of

that conversation, I'm like an eagle with binoculars: I see all. And I realize that those kids are picking on Rex.

I don't like bullies. I don't understand why you'd pick on someone instead of just . . . not picking on them, which is way easier. Still, I can't bend a bunch of fourth graders into balloon animals or I'm no better than Cameron Sykes.

So instead, I bellow from the library door, "Hey, Rex! Are you in there?"

"Indeed I am," Rex tells me.

"I've been trying to find you." I loom over the table like a big toe at a pinky toe convention. "Your buddy Cube told me you'd be here."

Rex blinks at me in confusion, because he knows I'm lying. But the other kids perk up, like

they can't believe that the star quarterback is friends with Rex.

"That assertion strikes me as—" he starts.

"Whoa!" I interrupt. "Cool briefcase. Is that a new one?"

"Ah, er," he says. "No, I'm afraid that my collection doesn't extend into the multiples."

Now *I* blink at *him* in confusion. Still, I manage to say, "Right! Well, c'mon, let's have lunch together."

"I should like that," he says. "However, my allotted time at the library has not yet elapsed."

"You mean you're supposed to stay here for a while?"

"Precisely."

"That's okay, Rex," Ms. Z says, shimmering into sight like a purple-headed angel. "Here's a pass. Have lunch early today."

See? Awesome.

So with the other fourth graders looking on, Rex goes to lunch with a sixth grader. And I don't know about your school, but at Blueberry Hill, that puts the *oo* in cool.

As we grab a couple of seats in the cafeteria, I ask Rex if he left the mops in place.

He says he did, and asks me if I've been studying the water cycle.

I say I haven't, and ask him if he's buying lunch today.

He says he isn't, and opens his briefcase an inch.

I hold my breath and wait to see what Mysterious Artifact emerges.

He pulls out a bag of barbecue potato chips.

Huh.

I want to ask what else is in the briefcase, but he's right about that whole none-of-your-business thing. So instead of asking, I start ranking potato chip flavors. We mostly agree, though Rex likes cool ranch, which is an abomination against salty snacks.

Then I give him half my tangerine and he starts talking about evaporation and condensation. Which reminds me that I'm supposed to be worrying about science class.

So I say, "Are you sure you put the mops in place?"

"I am quite hopeful," he says, "that *everything* is in place."

I almost ask what he means but decide instead to raise a broader, more philosophical question.

I'm in social studies now. After that, there's twenty minutes of Quiet Study and then science class. Complete with the dreaded science *test*.

MY QUIET STUDY TIMETABLE

2 minutes: grab the mops and race upstairs

+ 4 minutes: start a flood from the water fountain

+ 3 minutes: mop into the supply closet

+ 1 minute: unlock the cabinet with a 5 and a 4 and a 3 and a 2

+ 2 minutes: find the test answers

+ 7 minutes: memorize them

+ 8 seconds: forget them
+ 4 minutes: re-memorize them
+ 1 minute: race to science class
    before second bell
_____
= 20 minutes-ish? I don't know, math
    isn't my subject.

In general, students have two choices for Quiet Study.

1) Stay in class and doodle on a
    worksheet, or
2) Go to the multipurpose room
    and work with a study buddy.

However, I'm going with:

3) Sneak to the third floor and
    break into a supply closet.

So after social studies, I slink toward the stairwell. When I turn the corner, I find the mops that Rex propped in a bucket. I almost cheer. I've never been so happy to see cleaning supplies.

"Hey, Alley," Chowder says, as Maya leads him closer.

"Are you ready?" I ask.

"Of course we are!" Maya says. "We owe Rex for helping with our game."

Chowder's pupils turn into glittery pink hearts. "*Our* game."

"That's right." Maya raises her phone. "And he'll teach me Diamond Magic if I do one more favor for him."

"C'mon, you dorkfish!" I tell them. "Let's go!"

So we grab mops and—

Rex filled the bucket with water! Why the dripping heck did he do that? So now we're stuck carrying soaked mops upstairs, and leaving a trail of splashes behind us.

And as if that's not bad enough, I hear grunting from down the hall: *"Hut, hut, hut."*

"Cameron Sykes!" I hiss.

"What about him?" Chowder asks.

"He's coming this way!"

"He's like a swamp ogre," Maya says. "Who makes third graders cry for violating the dress code."

"Is he even on duty right now?" Chowder asks.

"He's a *vigilante* hall monitor," I say. "We can't let him see us!"

"Hut, hut, hawt, hawt." Sheesh. Cameron is such a flaming nostril that he can't even say "hut" right. *"Hawt, hawt!"*

We race upstairs. *"Hawt, hawt, hawt."*

We bounce off a wall. *"Hawt, hawt, HAWT!"*

We scramble up higher. . . .

Silence!

We pause on the landing, and there's no sound except our mops dripping onto the floor.

"I think we lost him," Chowder says.

"This never happens to snake soldiers," Maya grumbles.

"Okay, let's—" I say.

"*Hawt, hawt!*" the stairwell says.

We rocket up the next flight of stairs. At least we try to. But the landing is slippery from our dripping mops.

We slip, we slide, we crash.

We tangle together like earbuds in a pocket. Maya's left foot wedges into my armpit, and Chowder's left armpit clamps onto my face.

"*Hawt! Hawt!*"

We scramble behind a stack of chairs on the landing. It's *almost* the perfect place to hide.

On the bright side, we're concealed from view. That's a good thing in a hiding spot.

On the dimmer side, the floor is covered in confetti. That's *not* a good thing in a hiding spot . . . because when we dive into place, seventeen million blue flecks billow into the air.

Why? Why is *confetti* tucked behind a stack of chairs in the stairwell?

That's exactly the question I don't ask myself as I leap around like a hyperactive popcorn kernel, flapping my hands at the tiny bits of paper.

"*Hawt, hawt . . .*" The grunting fades away. "*Hawt. Hawt. Hawt.*"

"He's gone!" Maya says, from inside a cloud of confetti. "We're home free."

And, weirdly, she's right. We crawl from behind the chairs, and a minute later we reach the third floor. We did it!

We creep down the hallway, mops ready. I find the supply closet and prepare to clog the water fountain. . . .

Except there is no water fountain.

I groan. "Not *again*!"

There are fewer water fountains in this hallway than there were cabinets in the teachers' lounge. And this time, there isn't even a rectangle on the wall.

But there *is* a bucket sitting on a cafeteria tray. It's full to the brim, too. So without even thinking—which is sort of my thing—I splash the water across the floor.

Except the bucket is broken . . .

Look at that picture closely. Do you notice anything strange?

I mean other than the fact that we're now wetter than a whale's underpants? You don't, do you? Well, I'll tell you: that water is *cold*.

There is a brief intermission for shrieking and shivering, and then I stammer, "I'll p-push the water under the door. Maya, you f-find a teacher to open the lock and—"

And when my mop knocks into the door, it swings open.

"It's already unlocked," Chowder says.

"The Realm is with us!" Maya calls, and slips inside.

I bump into her when I follow. It's about as roomy as a hot dog bun in here, and I'm the second frank. But there, on the far wall, is a cabinet with a keypad lock! I'm not saying it glows with a heavenly light, but I'm not saying it doesn't, either.

Then Chowder bumbles inside and slams the door.

"Why'd you close the door?" Maya asks him, switching on her phone's flashlight.

"I didn't!" Chowder says. "Why'd you turn on the fan?"

"I didn't!" she says.

"What fan?" I ask, and wind blasts me from a fan in the corner.

Freezing wind, because I'm drenched with cold water.

We huddle together for warmth, and Chowder clears his throat. *Oh no.* He's going to recite a poem.

"Chowder, *don't!*" I beg him.

"You chase away goblins," he tells Maya, "with balls of icy fie-ah. You are sweeter than a gummy papaya. You asked me on this date to—"

"This isn't a date!" she says, filming the room with her phone. "I only asked you along so Rex would teach me Diamond Magic."

Chowder blinks a few times. "That's the—the only reason?"

"Yeah. Diamond Magic is legendary."

"My love," he announces, "is dead."

"Okay," Maya says.

Chowder sighs brokenheartedly, but I don't have time to comfort him right now. Instead, I reach for the cabinet—and two bizarre things happen in a row. I mean, two completely shocking events.

First, I remember the combination: 5-4-3-2.

Second, when I punch in the numbers, the cabinet opens.

Just like that.

A rainbow shines from inside the cabinet.

An angel sings.

I don't *actually* think the Golden Keys are binders made of solid gold, but maybe a little. Except when the rainbow fades, my gaze falls upon . . . school supplies.

Staples. Erasers. Boxes of sticky notes, helpfully labeled.

I have two questions.

First, why is this stuff locked away? There are school supplies in every classroom. Why force an innocent sixth grader to memorize a mind-boggling combination to break into a cabinet when there's nothing worthwhile inside?

Which brings me to my second question:
WHERE
ARE
THE
GOLDEN
KEYS?

I know they're in here somewhere! I dig into that cabinet like a hungry Labrador on Milk-Bone Beach. I fling rulers and tape dispensers around, and still don't find the Golden Keys.

"Quiet Study is over," Chowder tells me, picking stickies out of his hair. "We need to go."

"Not yet!" I say.

"C'mon, Alley," Maya says, sending messages on her phone. "We're late for class."

"One second," I say, narrowing my eyes.

"What're you doing?" Chowder asks.

"I'm *trying* to think."

"That's never worked before," Maya says.

"Hold on, hold on! I've almost got it."

A thought is swirling beneath the surface of my brain like a shark about to attack.

First there's just a ripple. Then there's a fin.

Then my eyes pop open and I stare at the school supplies.

"Pink stickies!" I announce. "Green stickies!"

"Uh," Chowder says.

"Yellow stickies!" I cry, then point to one more box. "And what is *that*?"

"Golden stickies?" Maya asks.

"Golden," I repeat, "stickies."

"Um," she says.

"Do you remember the last time you were stuck inside a locker?" I ask her.

"I've never been stuck inside a locker," she says.

For a moment, I forget my problems and stare at her. How do you reach sixth grade without once getting stuck in a locker? But that's not the point. "When you're in a locker," I inform her, "noises outside sound muffled."

"Yeah?"

"So if a teacher says 'golden stickies,' what would you hear?"

"Golden . . ." Maya whispers a syllable, then finishes: "—KIES."

"Golden Keys!" Chowder says, awed by my detective skills.

I'm a little awed too. For once, I understand everything. The Golden Keys don't exist. I mis-heard that teacher. This whole thing is a wild-goose chase. I'm pretty pleased with myself. . . .

Until Chowder says, "They're going to send you to Steggles for sure."

My heart stops.

The test!

The deadline!

If I don't get an A, my life turns into a horror movie.

Even as I stand in that cramped closet, I can hear toenail clippers going *click, click, click*. I catch a whiff of calf's-foot jelly, and on the cursed lawns of Steggles Academy, undead squirrels jerk to life. Hungry for acorns—and vengeance.

This is bad.

This so bad that my entire life flashes before my eyes:

What? No. What even *is* that? Why is a—

"Uh, Alley?" Maya says. "I just got a text from Rex. He says you need to get to class *now*. Like now now NOW now. Or you'll get a zero."

So I burst from the supply closet. "I'm on the way!"

"You're already too late!" Chowder shouts back.

But I'm not. Not if I get downstairs faster than anyone's ever downstairs-gotten before. And I know exactly how to do that.

This time, the idea doesn't swirl beneath the surface like a shark. This time, the idea leaps from the water, jaws wide and teeth gleaming.

In other words, I snatch up the cafeteria tray and launch myself downstairs.

"Extreme Schooling" for the win.

Let's talk about choices for a second. The problem with bad choices is that they *look* like good choices. They look like awesome choices. For example, if the fastest way to reach the first floor is tray-surfing, then of course you should surf a tray!

That's just common sense. And yet when I

reach the first floor, Cameron Sykes is standing in front of me like a traffic cop, blocking my way.

"NO HORSEPLAY IN THE HALLWAY!" he bellows, gesturing with his phone for me to turn away.

So my choices are:

1) Crash into Cameron, possibly
   lopping off his dumb head
   with a cafeteria tray.
2) Swerve sideways, allowing
   his dumb head to remain
   unlopped.

And I only have a split second to decide! Maybe I choose right, maybe I choose wrong. I still don't know for sure. There are good arguments on both sides.

But at the very last moment, I swerve.

I zoom sideways, in the direction Cameron is pointing. Toward that robotic JELL-O-butt that *someone* left in the lobby, and—

The good news: Ms. Li gives me fifteen minutes to clean up.

The bad news: After that, I'm stuck at my desk, staring at the science test.

I should probably read the questions, but I'm too busy trying not to cry. Trying not to think about living with Grannie Blatt, leaving Blueberry Hill, never seeing my friends again.

When the other kids hand in their tests, I gaze at my empty answer sheet. Is there a grade worse than an F? I might actually get a G on this.

I drag myself to Ms. Li's desk. "Um . . ."

"What is this, Alley?" she asks. "Why did *you* take the test?"

I heave a tragic sigh. "I know, right? Tests are

a terrible way to measure student performance."

"No, I mean because you signed up to give a presentation."

I heave an even tragic-er sigh. "I should have, but I didn't."

"Of course you did." She consults a list. "Oh! I guess your HOST signed you up."

"R-Rex?" I stammer. "Rex signed me up to give a presentation?"

"That's right."

"How? Who? When?"

"Right now," she says.

"But—but *why*?"

"He told me you prepared for this."

"Me!" I babble. "Prepared! For *this*!"

"I'm glad to hear it," Ms. Li says. "Now get started."

So I shuffle to the front of the class. I look across the sea of faces, praying for a lightning strike of brilliance. Or a lightning strike of *lightning*. I'd happily turn into a pile of ashes right now.

I say, "Uh, the water cycle . . ."

There's a long silence.

". . . is not Aquaman's exercise bike," I finish.

A few kids giggle.

"What can I say about the water cycle?" I ask, pacing in front of the blackboard.

"Good question!" a kid calls from the back.

"Yes, it is! And another good question is, 'Why are there so many kinds of cheese?'"

Ms. Li says, "Alley!"

"I believe Alley forgot his notes," Rex calls, and that's when I spot bunny ears at the projector.

"Muh?" I say.

"Thus, we shall use his recorded presentation," Rex says.

"Guh?" I say.

Ms. Li says, "That's fine," and turns off the lights.

Rex starts the projector and the screen says: *The Water Cycle by Alex Katz*.

"The water cycle has no beginning and no end!" my voice booms.

For a second, I don't know how I'm saying that. Then I remember: Rex made me repeat

science facts! He recorded me, and now he's playing it back.

"The water cycle is powered by the sun, which warms the oceans," my voice says, while in the background, another voice chants, *"Hawt, hawt, hawt, hawt . . ."*

A video starts playing on the screen. A video that rocks me to the very core:

I'm stunned and befuddled. Heck, I'm A+ fuddled. What is happening right now? The classroom seems to tilt around me while my voice babbles things like, "Vapor rises into the atmosphere" and "Next comes condensation," and Cameron Sykes chants, *"Hawt, hawt, hawt."*

After a horrible eternity, the video shows me bursting from the storage closet and tray-surfing downstairs. My voice says, "Precipitation falls from the sky as snow, sleet, rain, or—"

SMASH! I crash into the Jell-O—and my recorded voice howls, "Runoff! *Weeyow!* Smack-down monsoon storm cycle!"

And that's when Ms. Li turns on the lights.

There is a moment of silence.

A long, sticky moment of silence.

Then the cheering starts.

The entire class bursts into applause.

Wild, stamping, whistling applause—for *me*.

Kids whoop and chant, "All-ey! All-ey! All-ey!"

And I sway in shock. What is happening right now? Is this real? Who is what? How is where? When did why?

"Now *that*," Ms. Li tells me, "is a presentation nobody will ever forget!"

"A guh?" I say, because even my tongue is confused.

"Rex told me that you'd put on a real show," she says, chuckling. "And wow, did you deliver."

"I did?" I blink at her. "I mean, I did!"

"With Rex's help, of course. He forwarded the video that Maya took and . . ."

She keeps talking while realizations crackle in my brain like popping candy. Rex is behind this whole thing! *That's* the favor he asked from Maya: to send him video for my presentation. He saved me.

"Rex is made of magic," I tell Ms. Li. "He's a leprechaun with velvety ears. He's a crystal ball with a cottontail. He's a . . ."

"Paper towel?" Rex asks, suddenly beside me.

"No, you mopsy genius!" I beam at him. "You're not a paper towel!"

He offers me paper towels. "There is Jell-O behind your ears."

"Oh!" I gaze at him in wonder. "Do you think of *everything*?"

"I'm afraid not. However, I do attempt to anticipate the most likely eventualities."

"Like a boss," I say.

"Why don't you help Alley clean up a little more?" Ms. Li asks him.

"I would be happy to," Rex tells her, and leads me to the bathroom.

"You planned that whole thing!" I say, digging Jell-O out of my ears.

"I did," he admits.

"How did you know I wouldn't find the Golden Keys?"

He hands me another paper towel. "I suspected that your faith in their existence was misplaced."

"Well, you're wrong about *that*," I tell him. "They aren't even real."

"I stand corrected," he says.

"Yeah, I was surprised too. The whole thing was a misunder—wait! You sabotaged the water bucket, right?"

"I did."

"So we'd all squeeze together in that closet, like molecules in the atmosphere?"

"That is correct," he says.

"And you stuck the fan on high!"

"Indeed."

"How did you get Cameron's video of me hitting the Jell-O?"

"He uploads all student infractions to the website."

"Oh, yeah. What a creep." I wipe my neck. "So did you also scatter that confetti behind the chairs?"

Rex nods. "Raindrop-shaped confetti, to better approximate evaporation."

"Raindrop-shaped! You absolute Einstein!" I think for a second. "Okay, but how'd you know Cameron would chase us yelling, 'Hut, hut, hut'?"

"That was not Cameron yelling, 'Hut, hut, hut,'" he says. "That was *me*, intoning, 'Hot, hot, hot....'"

For a moment, I reel in bewilderment. Why would he do that? Then a bright light burns through the gloom of my confusion.

"Because the hot sun powers the water cycle!" I say, slam-dunking a soggy paper tower into the trash. "The sun provides energy for the lazy bodies of water—me, Alley, and Maya sweating in a heap in gym class!—to rise high in the atmosphere, the *staircase*, before squeezing together and tumbling back down!"

"Alley Katz," Rex says, giving a little bow. "You've mastered the water cycle."

26

Principal Kugelmeyer calls me into her office. She doesn't speak; she just looks at me.

Seconds tick past. I squirm in my chair, thinking about the mop mess and the water-bucket mess and the Jell-O mess.

Finally she says, "How do you explain *this*?" and turns her computer toward me.

And Principal Kugelmeyer shows me my grade: A+.

"I knew you could do it," she says, after my parents log off.

"I couldn't," I tell her. "Not without Rex."

She smiles. "The HOST program is good, right?"

"Even better than an alien invasion."

"I'm pleased to hear that. It's important that students learn to help each other."

"Like it says in the name," I remind her. "Helping Other Students Thrive."

"Sometimes, though," she says, "one student might need help academically, while another student needs help socially."

She's lost me, but I say, "Sure."

"A new kid in school, for example, might need someone to look out for him."

"That *is* an example," I agree.

"A young student who doesn't fit in, say."

I say, "Mm," to show that I'm listening.

"A kid so bright that he skipped two grades."

"Two grades!" I repeat, when she pauses for a response.

"Yes. Perhaps a student who doesn't . . . dress like the other children. A boy who would benefit from the friendship of an older, more popular student."

I have no clue what she's talking about, so I say, "Correct-a-mundo."

Then I start thinking about brownies and oranges. How come so few foods are named after colors? It's a better system than most food names. Maybe I'll start calling milk "white" and bananas "yellows" and—

"Alley. Alley." Principal Kugelmeyer's voice breaks into my thoughts. "Alley!"

"Here!" I say. "Present! Hello!"

"How much of that did you miss?"

"Honestly? Everything after I sat down."

She looks stern for a second, then snorts a laugh. "Oh, just go away! Go be yourself."

"That's my best subject," I tell her.

"Oh, but one more thing," she says, when I'm at the door. "Do you want to keep Rex as a HOST?"

"You mean, like, permanently?"

She looks worried, for some reason. "You don't have to, but I think it might—"

"Sign me up," I tell her. "That kid's my lucky rabbit's foot."

This is my school. Ordinary buses. Ordinary trees. Ordinary kids.

Not him. He's *extra*ordinary.

Well, he still doesn't know how to shake hands, but he's young. If he sticks with me, he'll learn a thing or two.

So I'm still at Blueberry Hill with my friends. I'm not trimming anyone's wart hairs, I'm not clipping anyone's toenails. I'm not eating calf's-foot jelly.

I'm still making a lot of choices . . . and not all of them are bad.